The Bitty Twins' Bedtime Story

Written by Jennifer Hirsch
Illustrated by Stephanie Roth

Please, please, read one more story!

No more stories. Time for bed.

Shhh, I have a good idea—
we'll make a story up instead.
Come get underneath the covers.
Ready? Okay, here we go:

Once upon a time there was
a queen who lived in a big rainbow.
One day the queen—

Wait, you forgot about the king who lived there, too.

Okay. One day the queen *and* king were trying to think of things to do—

And then the king had a great idea! He said, "Let's go out for a ride in our new race cars." They got in and started driving side by side.

A race car? I don't think the queen
would drive a car. I'll tell you why:
this queen would rather ride a horse—
a magic horse, one that can fly!

And so they flew—and drove—together,
through the rainbow and the sky.
At last they landed on a cloud.

"Let's take a rest," the queen said. "I am getting sleepy. How 'bout you?"

"I'm never sleepy," said the king.
"But I am hungry."

Said the queen,
"We have no food here,
that's the thing."

Suddenly, they heard some thumping
coming from beneath the cloud.
They listened to the sound—what was it?
Footsteps, growing awful loud . . .

The king said, "It must be a giant!"

"A scary giant?" asked the queen.

"Yes, probably," the king replied.
"Most giants are kind of mean."

"Let's get back to our rainbow—hurry!"
The king zoomed off in his racing car.
The queen leapt on her flying horse
and galloped to a far-off star.

Clunk, clunk! Clunk, clunk!
Hear the footsteps
of the giant coming close . . .
Are you scared, too?

No, just hungry.
Odd—this giant
smells like toast.

Knock, knock, knock.
It's the giant, come to launch a big attack!

Hello in there—
I heard some noise.
Would you two like
a bedtime snack?

The king and queen had toast and milk,
and so their story ended right.

The giant smoothed
their rumpled rainbow,

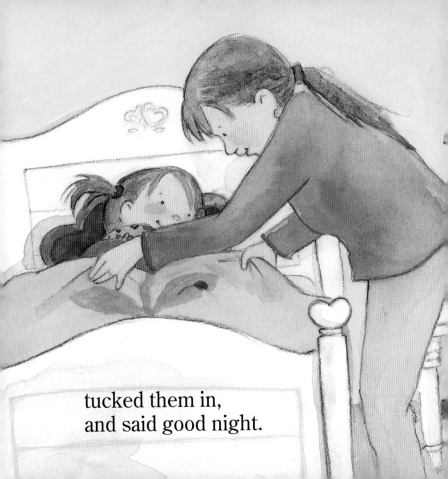

tucked them in,
and said good night.

Dear Parents . . .

Every child loves a bedtime story. While there are many wonderful children's books, *telling* a story instead of reading one has some delightful advantages: you can create characters and situations just for your child—and she can listen in the dark, letting her imagination bring the story to life while her body prepares for sleep.

Share Old Favorites

Start out by retelling classics, such as *The Little Red Hen*, *The Princess and the Pea*, or *Goldilocks and the Three Bears*. They may seem old hat to you, but they'll feel fresh to her. Tell them in your own words, and don't worry if you can't remember the details—just make up new ones. In fact, once you gain confidence as a storyteller, you can change things deliberately. How about Goldilocks and the three gorillas? Or Goldilocks and the three little pigs? Don't be afraid to mix things up and get silly—your little one will love it!

What If?

A fun approach to storytelling is to take a simple aspect of daily life and change one major detail: "One day, a new family moved into the house next door. Except it turned out they weren't people—they were kangaroos." How the kangaroos next door go about their everyday lives—eating, getting dressed, going to school—will be an endless source of fascination and humor for your child. Don't be surprised if bedtime becomes something she really looks forward to!

A Story Just for Her

What's going on in your daughter's life? Does she have a new friend? Then tell a story about two little girls (with the names of your daughter and her friend, of course) and their marvelous trip to the zoo—or to the moon. Is she worried about you traveling out of town for a few days? Make up a story about a mommy or daddy who goes away. Tell all about the interesting things that happen and the joyful reunion when the mommy or daddy returns home.

A Story Just for You

Some nights, let *her* tell *you* a story. Her tale will give you insights into what she's thinking about and how she solves problems— a peek into the mind and world of your daughter.

The Moral of the Story

Is there something you'd like your young one to get better at, such as brushing her teeth or putting away her toys? Make up a fable (like the famous ones by Aesop) that teaches the specific lesson you need—for example, the little beaver who wouldn't brush his teeth and got a toothache; or messy Marissa moth, who couldn't go out flying because she couldn't find her wings. Just make sure the main character solves the problem successfully, for a happy ending.